On the wings of a butterfly

?

Amelia K Oliver

On the wings of a butterfly

Amelia K Oliver

Published by Amelia K Oliver, 2020.

This is a work of fiction. Similarities to real people, places, or events are entirely coincidental.

ON THE WINGS OF A BUTTERFLY

First edition. June 6, 2020.

Copyright © 2020 Amelia K Oliver.

Written by Amelia K Oliver.

Dedicated to my auntie Barbara and auntie Andrea, whom both fought cancer with dignity and grace, but sadly cancer won. To my aunt Shirley, who has fought this awful disease several times and continues to be the victor. To all men, women and children who fight, you're all in my heart. I'd also like to dedicate this to the scientists working hard to beat cancer. Thank you for all that you do.

Chapter One

July 1st

The bus was tightly packed with people just trying to get home after a gruelling day at work. Jessica coughed into her hand, attempting to be polite in the middle of the packed bus. If she was getting sick, she didn't want to spread it around. Hot liquid sprayed her palm so she wiped it on the leg of her pants and thought no more of it.

"Excuse me, " she tapped the man in front of her on the shoulder, "I need to get past." He didn't acknowledge her at all. She tried again but the tall, brawny man didn't hear her. She let out a soft sigh as the bus driver sped past her stop. She would need to run back, her mum needed her meds and Jessica was determined to not let her down. When she was just fourteen, Jessica became a full-time carer for her mum. The burden was heavy, but one she carried with a lot of love. She was determined to get to the nursing home before her mother had time to worry. It was dark outside, colder than it should be for July. Her thin coat and the many people around her didn't stop the chill from seeping into her bones, making her shiver. The man reached his hand out to press the button, the bell rang out and the driver signaled he was about to turn into the next stop. Jessica smiled, she could finally get off the bus and get to her mum.

She shuffled forward, strangers pressed into back, urging her forward. As she stepped out onto the pavement, Jessica felt another cough work it's way up her throat. The white paper bag in her hand rustled as she stumbled, her foot slid off the metal step. As she fell through the air, Jessica coughed again. Blood shot out of her mouth, spraying a red mist around her. She was unconscious before she hit the ground.

Chapter two

July 2nd

Jessica peeked her eyes open only to slam them shut again. The lights above her seared her eyes, making them water. A tear escaped, rolled down her cheek and landed on the softness behind her. A deep masculine voice spoke, making Jessica freeze.

"Jessica?"

When she opened her eyes again, they met a rich, dark brown pair. His skin was dark, too. A golden brown, it reminded Jessica of the forest floor after a summer rain. His lips were full and soft looking. He was clean shaven. His pristine white doctor's coat sported his name tag which read Dr A. Wilkie.

"Yes, that's me." She replied and tried to sit up but couldn't. She looked down at her arm where a needle was buried deep within her skin. "What the, " words failed her. The last thing Jessica remembered was stepping off the bus.

"Fluids, they'll help you feel a little better. You're doing just fine, Miss." The doctor said softly, his tone soothed as it wrapped around her, offering her comfort.

"What happened? I was on the bus, " her hand flew to her mouth as a memory played behind her eyes. "I fell, didn't I?"

"Yes, but you suffered only minor injuries. Some bruising, too. Our tests, however, showed some troubling news," The man paused to look down at the clipboard in his hands, "Ms Admiral, is there anyone we can call? Someone to be with you?"

"No, no, my mum has dementia. She lives in assisted living. There's no one else." Jessica frowned, "I'd like to sit up, if that's ok?" Laying down in a strange room with a strange man next to her gave Jessica the hebby-jebbies. But something about him also soothed her. The twinkle in his eyes spoke to her.

"Of course, I'll get someone," the man smiled softly and rose from the stool he sat on and walked to the door. Staring at the ceiling, Jessica counted her limbs.

All there. The thought thankfully. *But everything hurt.*

He poked his head out and looked up and down the hall.

"One moment, Ms Admiral," he said and disappeared through the opening.

Glancing around, Jessica could tell from where she lay in a private room. No other noises reached her as she waited for the doctor to come back. A small window in the wall beside her let only a minute amount of light through it, making the room appear gloomy and depressing. Jessica hated hospitals. They reminded her of when her dad had a heart attack and shortly after passed away. It only took six months after being diagnosed for her mother to decline to the point where Jessica could no longer look after her. She had no good memories of these places.

"I'm sorry, " the doctor strode back into the room. "All the nurses are busy. I can help you sit up, though," he said as he stood over her, a warm smile on his face.

"Okay." Jessica steeled herself as he bent and worked his hand behind her back. Her whole body hurt, sitting up was going to be painful. Gently, excruciatingly, the doctor helped her sit up. By the time she laid back on the pillows he placed behind her, Jessica was out of breath and tears gathered in her eyes.

"I'm sorry." The doctor said for what had to be the millionth time since he walked back into the room. What he had to be sorry for she had no idea.

"I'm ok," she assured him even though she could hardly contain how much she hurt.

Minor injury? I feel like the bus hit me, never mind I only fell off it.

The Doctor sat back down on the tiny seat by her bed. Jessica turned slightly so she could look into his handsome face.

He is far too handsome to be a doctor. She thought as she took in his features. Jessica shook herself, remembering she was in a hospital bed, not on a date.

"So, what was wrong with your tests, Doc?" She tried to add a little humour into her words but the pain that had plagued her for the last six months, added to the new pain from the fall, meant there was little humour to be found.

"Jessica, " he took her hand in his. Hers felt cold and soft in his hot, rough ones. Oddly, she found that comforting. "I'm so sorry to be the one to tell you this but," he paused, obviously trying to select the right words. "You have stage four ovarian cancer. It has spread to other organs." He paused again, allowing his words to sink in, "Jessica, I'm so sorry, but it's terminal."

Chapter Three

"Terminal? Like, I'm dying?" Jessica could hardly believe what she was hearing. She sat forward and pulled her hand from beneath the Doctor's, leant her elbows on her knees and rested her head in her hands. Her confusion masking the pain.

This can't be right. It just can't.

Seven months ago she went to the doctor, complaining of a stomach ache. At first, he told her it was irritable bowel syndrome, he gave her medication and sent her home. Weeks later, the pain intensified, so she went again. A hernia, he had told her. But there was no funding left in the area for the operation. He prescribed painkillers and told her to avoid heavy lifting. Which was impossible because she had to take care of her mum. The pain radiated out from her stomach, spreading to other parts of her body. Every time she sought help, she was told the same thing. There is no funding.

"Wait, are you telling me the pain in my stomach isn't a hernia, but in fact it's cancer?" Jessica asked without looking at the doctor.

"Yes, I'm so very sorry, Jessica ." the doctor replied, his tone sincere. Jessica stiffened as he placed his hand on her back and rubbed in circles. Her mind whirled and her stomach revolted.

Turning to the side, Jessica emptied the contents of her stomach onto the floor, her eyes squeezed closed at the horror she saw below.

Crimson.

Stark against the white floor. Despite closing her eyes, she still saw the mess her body expelled behind her eyelids.

A flurry of activity barely registered as Jessica's mind shut down.

Cancer.

Terminal.

I'm going to die.

Jessica was only thirty-two. She had no children, no husband, she had never seen the rush to settle down. She thought she had time for all of that. Now suddenly, she was out of time.

I haven't even lived, yet.

More vomit worked its way up her throat and as it flew from her mouth and nose, black spots dotted over her vision. The pain in her body rose to an unbearable level as if to tell her *I told you something was wrong and you ignored me!*

Jessica fell unconscious, the doctor's face the last thing she saw.

Chapter Four

July 3rd

"Jessica, wake up, love." Andy Wilkie gently shook her shoulder. It was nine am and the sun shone through the window beside her bed, highlighting the red tones in her hair. The covering on the window cast a golden shine over her skin, giving her a healthy glow. But Andy knew she was deathly pale.

Even sick, she's beautiful. Andy's errant thought shocked him. He had never once had a thought like this about a patient. So why now?

Her azure eyes fluttered open, her lashes like the wings of a butterfly against her cheeks. Andy knew he shouldn't notice Jessica was a beautiful woman, given she was his patient, but he couldn't stop himself. She was a vision of beauty.

"Uh, I need to pee in the worst way, Doc." Jessica 's voice was gravelly from not being used for hours and her throat felt like a dried up prune.

"You're bagged, love. Pee, it's fine." Andy replied, a smile in his voice.

Jessica 's eyes flicked to his earthy brown ones. Something was different. But she couldn't put her finger on what.

"If it's all the same, Doc, I'd like to pee like normal, if that's ok?" She raised her eyebrow at him in a challenge. If he was going to stand in the way of her and the toilet, he risked being peed on.

"Okay, I'll get a nurse," Andy replied, laughing softly as he left the room. Andy wanted to confess he spent the last day at her bedside as much as he could. Watching her chest rise and fall, willing her to live.

I might freak her out, if I tell her. Better not. His day off was usually spent relaxing at home. Alone. But something about this woman intrigued him to the point he was willing to give her his free time.

Within minutes, Jessica was free of tubes and sitting on a cold toilet seat, peeing like a horse. The nurse insisted she stand behind the door, her foot wedged between the door and the frame, just in case.

"Just in case I kick the bucket on the bog, Nurse?" Jessica called from the throne, barely stifling a wince as her nether region stung.

Son of a biscuit eater, did they use a drain pipe for a catheter? She thought as she went about her business.

"In case you need assistance, Sweetie." The woman kindly called back.

Jessica rolled her eyes. "I've not needed assistance since I was two, but thanks." The nurse giggled. So did Jessica. Finishing up, Jessica waddled to the sink and splashed water over her face. When she looked up, the woman in the mirror stared back with shocked eyes.

Before her mother got sick, Jessica was a plump woman. When she complained to her mother about it, she always replied

"Men like women with a bit of shape, Dear." to which she would always reply,

"Round is a shape, right?" They would giggle about it and Jessica would forget all her problems. Her mother, Renee, had the biggest heart Jessica had ever known. Always laughing and making jokes, the woman was Jessica's idol. When she started to forget things, Jessica picked up the pieces. She forgot about dating and dieting went out of the window. Now, her cheekbones stuck out, her eyes were sunken and the open-backed hospital gown hung off her frame.

The cancer diet, I wouldn't recommend it. Jessica shook her head and attempted to close the back of her gown. *Arse on show, puking my guts out... awesome.*

She padded back into the room to find the nurse gone but the doctor sitting on the edge of her bed.

"What's up, Doc?" She quipped and moved to sit on the chair beside the Doctor, giggling at her own joke.

"We have to talk, Jessica ." Andy hated to do it, but he didn't believe Jessica understood the full details of her sickness.

"Uh oh, nothing good ever came after that sentence, Doc. How about this, " Jessica held the two pieces of cloth behind her back, "you tell me when I can go home and we can just leave it like that, yeah?" Jessica said seriously.

"I'm afraid not." Andy, for the first time in his career, was genuinely tempted to do just that. But he had a duty to fulfil, and, even though he knew he shouldn't, Andy cared for Jessica. "I wish I could, but you need to be informed." He slid off the bed and strode to the small window. For a moment he simply looked out, the view of the garden was stunning from this height, it momentarily made him miss the cabin in the woods he spent every summer in as a kid.

"Ok, spit it out then." Jessica waved him on. She had things to do before she died. She had no time to waste here in this awful place.

Time is life, Doc.

"Your prognosis is not good. We estimate your life expectancy at a month, maybe six weeks," he said quietly, but Jessica heard him. "The cancer has spread to your lungs and stomach. You collapsed on the bus due to lack of oxygen."

She sat back on the chair, it's cold covering gave her a little shock as it made contact with her bare arse cheeks.

Six weeks. Well, shit. That's no time at all to cram sixty years into. Jessica thought as she started down at her dry hands.

"Oh." Was all she could manage.

"I'm so sorry, Jessica ." Andy repeated his regret over and over. He knew as her doctor, he couldn't wrap his arms around her like he wanted to. And he did really want to. He couldn't make it go away, as much as he wished he could. Andy was stuck leaning against the wall, his fists clenched in his pockets to prevent himself from punching the wall or pulling her to him and kissing her until her foot rose off the floor.

Keep your hands to yourself, Andy. She's vulnerable and in pain, now isn't the time or place. Andy repeated over and over in his mind.

"I'd like to be discharged immediately, please," Jessica demanded softly. After thirty-two years of being alive, it was time to start living.

My life isn't over yet.

Chapter Five

Andy watched from the golden tinted window as Jessica climbed shakily into a taxi. As her doctor, he signed the paperwork stating the patient wanted to live the rest of her life at home and would come back for treatment. The type of treatment he would be forced to tell her could prolong her life, like he was forced to tell his other cancer patients. But it would only make her last few weeks on earth hellish.

Chemo was harsh, worse than the cancer. He didn't want that for Jessica. He didn't wipe away the tear slipping down his cheek as the taxi pulled away and took the first woman he had ever felt a connection with, away from him. He would never see her again. Andy knew her death would be a loss to this world. And to his.

Chapter Six

July 10th

Jessica walked from the flower shop, a bunch of daisies under her arm. The sun hung high in the sky, making everyone in Scarborough complain about how hot it was. But Jessica welcomed it. She tilted her face up to the sky, soaking up the sun's harmful rays, unafraid of the effects of wearing no sunscreen.

Skin cancer can bite my arse!

The smell of flowers reached her nose, making her take a deep breath. *It's amazing the things we take for granted when you think you've got a lifetime to live.* She thought as she walked slowly down the street, taking in the sights and sounds of the seaside town she called home her whole life.

Children ran loose, their shrill screams piercing everyone's ears within a mile. Jessica smiled, where she would have once been glad she didn't have any kids, now she only felt sadness. There were so many things she wouldn't get to do. *I didn't even realise I wanted children, until I was told I was dying. Go figure.* But there was nothing she could do about it now. Not with only weeks to live. No one was going to want to go out with a dying woman, let alone one in her thirties. The kind eyes of Dr Wilkie flashed in her mind and her heart constricted a little. If they had met under different circumstances he might have been someone she could have loved.

He's smart, compassionate. Handsome. Totally husband material. She shook her head knowing there were no other circumstances. He was a doctor and she was...nobody. And she was dying.

She headed for the cafe at the end of the pier, she and her mother loved to go to on Sunday's. It was their favorite spot to eat. Jessica sat on a bench overlooking the sandy beaches that stretched on for miles. The wind blew her hair around her face as she took a sip of coffee. She allowed herself to be distracted watching families enjoying the warm weather.

So much life to live. Every second precious. She didn't even notice when a man sat next to her until he cleared his throat.

"Oh! You made me jump," the words lodged in her throat when she spun round to come face to face with Doctor Wilkie. "It's you." She said so softly, the wind almost took the words away with it.

Chapter Seven

"It's me," Andy replied with a smile as he reached forward and tucked a strand of Jessica's hair behind her ear.

Jessica's cheeks flamed as the doctor's fingers brushed against her cheek.

"Got a day off, Doc? I thought you guys worked twenty-four seven." She giggled to mask the effect the contact had on her.

Down girl.

"Nightshift." He shrugged. They sat, staring into each other's eyes as a beautiful young waitress placed his coffee on the table in front of them, batting her lashes at Andy. Jessica was shocked when he didn't even look the girl's way.

Interesting. Maybe he's gay? That girl was smoking hot and not even a glance her way!

"Thanks." He said absently, feeling lost in Jessica's azure eyes. She looked well, considering her life was slipping through her fingers like sand. "How are you, Jessica?" He hadn't meant to ask, knowing full well it was none of his business. In all honesty, he hadn't been able to stop thinking about her these last few days. It was a happy coincidence he spotted her staring at the beach below.

Perhaps fate brought me here on this beautiful day to meet this beautiful woman?

"I'm good, thanks. My mum's house sold this morning, the money will be used to keep her in the nursing home until she passes away. So that's a blessing." Jessica smiled fondly. Her mother was her best friend. Knowing her mom would be taken care of when she died lifted a great weight from Jessica's shoulders.

"That's good. So, where are you staying?" Andy enquired, then took a sip of his coffee. It was bitter and cold. The way he felt for the last few days since Jessica walked out of his hospital and out of his life.

"Well, I decided to treat myself and book into the Village Hotel for a couple of nights." She replied, feeling slightly self-conscious. The doctor was incredibly handsome. Jessica felt like a leaf crushed under a boot.

A man like him would never go for a woman like me, especially since I'm on borrowed time.

"Love that place, the pool is amazing. Jessica, " Andy swallowed audibly, he was not a smooth man. He didn't do well with women. He was married to his career, not many women understood that, "I'd like to, " he paused, struggling to form the right words, "will you, erm, well,"

Jessica cut him off, her words laced with contempt.

"I don't need a pity date, Doc. But thanks." She stood, her movements jerky with anger.

As she turned to walk away, Andy leapt to his feet and grabbed her wrist. She spun, her eyebrows drawn down in a frown.

"It's not pity, Jessica, it's attraction. Admiration. A bit of lust, " he shrugged his shoulder, mentally slapping himself for that last bit. *Bloody hell!* "Let me try again." He let go of her and took a step back. Looking into her eyes, Andy asked, "Jessica, would you give me the immense honour of having tea with me?" oddly he added, "please." *Nerves were a bitch.*

Jessica threw her head back and laughed. The doctor was crazy, asking her out. *I'm dying, Doc, I have less than nothing to offer you.* But as her laughter died down she took in the serious look on his face, she realised he wasn't joking.

"Okay, Doc. But one condition, " Jessica teased.

"Anything." Andy found himself agreeing before he knew what she wanted.

"You tell me your name, first."

Chapter Eight

Jessica knocked on Andy's door and butterflies began to dance in her belly. She was twenty minutes late, the damn taxi driver took her the long way around, driving down the seafront instead of using the back roads. But she didn't mind too much, Scarborough was beautiful at night.

Andy stood behind his front door, mid internal panic attack. *She's here. Fuck, fuck, fuck.* As six o'clock came and went, he thought for sure she stood him up. Or worried her time had come earlier than he hoped. Estimates were not guarantees, after all. But when he heard the buzzer, the immense weight piled on his shoulders fell off and he breathed again. *Time to nut up, Andy. The woman of your dreams is behind this door. Open it!*

"Jessica," he uttered as he opened the door. She wore a knee-length flowery dress with a white cardigan draped over her shoulders. The small heels on her feet made her eyes level with his. Light makeup gave her a healthy look and the flowery scent of her perfume made his mouth water. Daisies.

Beautiful.

"Hey, Andy. Wanna let me in? It's freezing out here." She fake grumbled as Andy stared open-mouthed at her. She blushed under his gaze. He looked at her like Jessica looked at cake.

I love cake.

"Sorry! Please, come in." Andy moved out of the way so Jessica could step into his three-bedroom house.

Jessica could tell right away Andy had money. Everything in his house looked brand new. From the dark red leather sofa to the huge flatscreen on the wall. Its dark surface didn't have a single spec of dust on it. She couldn't help but wonder if he had a cleaning lady, or if he was OCD.

Or even has a wife?

Andy stood behind her and helped her slide off her cardigan, the tips of his fingers left goosebumps in their wake as they brushed over her soft skin. Both of them cleared their throats awkwardly. The effect the small contact was clear for them both.

"Drink?" He offered, his anxiety made his tone an octave higher than usual. He cleared his throat and tried again. "Tea, coffee? Or something cold?" Andy knew she couldn't drink on the pain meds she was on, so he made sure to stock up on soft drinks in preparation. The cupboard next to the sink was full of them, not knowing which she'd like, Andy bought one of each available.

"Got any róse? I skipped my meds so I could have a drink," Jessica paused, mentally kicking herself. "Not that I need to drink. I mean, this isn't torture or anything, so," she coughed into her hand. "A piece of rope, perhaps?" She joked. They both laughed, the tension broke. They both relaxed a bit as they walked down the hall.

"Yes, I have wine. Sit, let's get drunk, eh?" Andy said when he caught his breath.

Jessica sat on the sofa as Andy rushed off to get the wine and no doubt check on whatever was cooking in the kitchen.

Familiar smells wafted into the room, making her mouth water. She hadn't been very hungry lately but being here with Andy, feeling as normal as she had in a long time, she was suddenly famished. Seconds later, he presented her with a glass half full of delicious smelling wine.

"Cheers!" She giggled when he raised his glass to hers and clicked them together.

"Cheers." They laughed around mouthfuls of fruity liquid.

"I thought you were on the night shift?" Jessica asked over the rim of her glass, her eyes taking Andy in. He wore black jeans and a white shirt, his sleeves rolled up to his elbows. There was something about the forearms of a man that did things to her and Andy was certainly no exception.

Hotness overload.

"Yeah, I was. Took the night off." He replied casually. It was last minute but he made it work.

Work could wait for once.

"Nice. Dying of hunger here, Andy. What's for tea?" Jessica complained lightly, drawing a silly smile from him with one or her own.

"I went with the classics. Chips, garlic bread and for afters, " he paused for full effect, "cheesecake."

Jessica laughed heartily, a drop of wine dripped down her chin, Andy found his eyes riveted on it.

Would she nut check me if I licked it off? Yup, she would.

"Bloody hell, you've brought the big guns!" she giggled. Andy reached out and wiped the wine from her chin. Jessica swallowed thickly and as she met his earthy brown eyes, she felt flames of lust wash over her.

Andy smiled sheepishly then held out his hand as he rose

from his seat. Jessica took it. The wine went to her head, making her feel hot.

Or was it hot-doc?

Once in the dining room, Jessica was shocked to see takeaway boxes on a light oak table.

"Wow, you really did bring out the big guns, Andy!" Jessica giggled.

"Only the best for you, Milady." Andy quipped, "I'm a terrible cook, I didn't want to poison you on our first date." Andy admitted, then realised he had said the D-word. Date.

Oh, shit.

"A date, is it? Hmm, " Jessica tapped a red-tipped finger to her chin, cancer had all sorts of fun side effects. "Okay, but don't expect a night of passion after. I need at least a pepperoni pizza for that."

Andy walked over to the table and opened a box, revealing a pepperoni pizza. His smile was a mile wide. Jessica took another sip of wine to hide the blush on her cheeks.

Busted. Does that mean he's interested? Oh, God, I didn't shave! Jessica hid her anxiety well.

Andy and Jessica ate and drank. They laughed and joked. Having more fun than either of them had ever had. The hands on the black clock on the cream wall behind them sped towards midnight like a freight train on the loose. Neither of them noticed the passing of time or the fact they made their way through several more bottles of wine. By the time the clock struck one am, they were both drunk and exhausted. But beyond happy.

"Take the bed, Jessica, I'll sleep on the sofa. No biggie." Andy offered when Jessica said she was tired.

"You can share the bed, but no hanky panky, got it?" Jessica slurred as she took his hand and pulled him up the stairs.

Andy tried not to watch as Jessica undressed in the dark room. But he couldn't help it. Despite cancer having ravaged her body, she was still sexy.

The most beautiful woman I've ever seen.

They snuggled down together, Andy's arm around her waist.

I could die now, a happy woman. Jessica thought, feeling safe and content in Andy's arms. Within seconds, they were both asleep.

Chapter Nine

July 24th

Jessica stayed at Andy's house for four days and nights after their first night. They didn't talk about it, it just happened. He didn't ask her to leave, and she didn't ask to stay. Andy arranged to use his unspent holiday days so he could spend time with the woman who was quickly becoming the love of his life. They spent the time talking, getting to know each other. Andy couldn't deny the connection between them. Neither could Jessica. Each night they lay in bed, his arms wrapped tightly around her. He never once tried to have sex with her. They just fit, like the pieces of a puzzle. On the fourth day, they visited Jessica's mother.

"Mum, this is Andy." Jessica stood next to a small woman in her early seventies. Andy could tell they were mother and daughter by their matching smiles.

"Andy, is it? Well, when will there be grand babies and a wedding?" Her mother huffed, giving Andy a defiant glare.

"Does next week work for you?" Andy knelt in front of the elderly woman, "but what will Bruce Willis, your boyfriend, think?" Jessica's mother looked up at her with a smile on her face.

"I like him. But he'll have to put up with Brucy, " the nurses dotted around the large social space all looked in their direction as they laughed loudly.

"Oh, mum, you crack me up." Jessica smiled at Andy. It had been a long time since she saw her mum laugh so carefree. He was just the medicine they needed.

It's a shame there isn't a cure for cancer.

"Are you sure about this, Jessica? I mean," Andy looked over the edge of the bridge, the water below them was almost black except for the odd white wave.

"Absolutely, come on Andy, " Jessica wrapped her arms around his waist and pulled him close. "This was your idea, remember?" The wind chilled their faces as it whipped around them.

Despite not being a fan of heights, Andy agreed to do a bungee jump with her. Although they never talked about her sickness, they both knew her time was limited. He would deny her nothing, ever.

"I know." He ran his hands up the sides of her body. She had lost even more weight in the last two weeks. Despite his best efforts, she couldn't keep food down. Her ribs poked out, making the journey of his fingers a bumpy one. "Come on, then, let's throw ourselves off this bridge. because who doesn't find hurtling towards the ocean with only a bit of rope to keep you safe, fun?" Jessica smiled. She knew Andy hated heights but the fact that he was here with her, for her, meant more than a thousand words. She took his hand in here and stepped to the edge, their backs to the open air.

"Ready?" The instructor yelled. Andy and Jessica looked into each other's eyes and nodded. Andy's heart knew he wasn't agreeing to the jump. He was agreeing to love her forever. He was so in love with the woman next to him that it filled his every breath with joy. Just being around her gave him a whole new look on life.

He loved her. But he couldn't tell her.

Hand in hand, Andy and Jessica fell through the air. While she knew her life could end any day, she had never felt more alive. And neither had Andy.

July 25th

"Make love to me, Andy?" Jessica's lips brushed against his neck, making him shiver. He pulled back, his hands cupped her face.

"You are incredible, " his words were placed with so much love Jessica almost cried. She knew what she was doing was wrong. That taking this step with Andy would only hurt them both in the end. And the end was coming. She could feel it. His touch was gentle, loving as they slowly rose from the couch. Soft jazz played in the background as the two lost themselves in each other. For hours they kissed and touched, not a word was spoken. Their actions did all the talking for them. This was more than sex. It was more than love. It was something neither of them had a word for. No one did. There are a few times in life where two souls connect beyond what is usual. They become so in sync that making love becomes a spiritual act. That's what happened when Jessica gave herself to Andy and Andy gave himself in return.

They became one.

July 31st

Andy smiled down at Jessica as they danced under the lights of the gazebo. Her white dress could have passed for a wedding dress. Knee-length, it gave her curves where she no longer had curves. Her hair was pinned up, soft curls framed her face.

"You're so beautiful, love," Andy confessed as he held her close, "I'm a lucky guy." His eyes sparkled under the twinkling lights above them, his love for her shone bright.

"You sure are, Doctor Wilkie." Jessica teased. The night was warm and soft jazz played in the background. The charity event they were at faded into the background as he gazed into her eyes. "You don't look too bad yourself, Doc," Jessica said against his lips. The sweet kiss sent tingles down her spine. They swayed to the music. Their bodies touched from knees to their chests as *Bloodstream* by *Stateless* played in the background. Andy held her hand over his heart. It was perfect. She didn't know how long she had left but Jessica savoured every second she got with Andy.

He taught me how to live, just when I ran out of time.

Suddenly, Andy spun her. As she twirled, Jessica giggled like a schoolgirl. Ignoring the pain zipping through her body, she let Andy take over. Jessica felt like she was in a movie. This was not how she expected to spend the last few weeks of her life. She was in pain, that she expected. A lot of pain. What she wasn't prepared for was to fall in love with Andy. It was selfish of her, she knew, but she never meant for it to happen.

It just did.

"Jessica, I," Andy began, his throat dried up and the words lodged in his throat. He sank to one knee.

Jessica 's hand flew to her mouth, stifling the sob that left her. Tears sprang to her eyes and poured down her cheeks, unchecked.

"Andy, "

"Jessica, these last few weeks have been the happiest of my life. I love you, Jessica ." His hand shook as he reached into his pocket and pulled out a box. "Will you marry me?" he popped the lid off, revealing a light pink diamond set into a black band.

"Oh, Andy." Her legs felt like jelly beneath her. Andy must have felt it because he took her hip and pulled her down onto his knee. Perched there, Jessica could hardly form a thought.

Marry him? He loves me? Me?

"Before you say anything, know this, I don't care if I have you for a day, a week, an hour. I want you, Jessica, for however long I can have you. Mind, body and soul, I am yours, forever, even after death. I will meet you there, my love. I want nothing more than to make you my wife, to love you and cherish you with every breath you take. You're the one, Jessica, I've searched for you my whole life, and now I have you, I don't want to let you go. You're the love of my life. Say you'll me mine, Jessica?" Andy meant every word. That much was obvious. Jessica could almost feel his love radiate off him.

Her tears dried on her skin as she looked deep into his eyes, searching for any indication he had doubts. Finding nothing but love there, Jessica leant forward and pressed her lips to Andy's. When she pulled away, Andy's whole body froze.

"I'm so sorry, Andy." She rose to her feet, nausea rolled through her. "No." Jessica walked as fast as she could in the opposite direction. She didn't know where she was going, but she kept going anyway. She couldn't do this to him. Force him to watch her die horribly. She refused to allow him to waste his life on her. She didn't have long left, she knew. Her heart broke into a million pieces, like a mirror. Pieces of her fluttered in the wind, lost forever.

She loved him too. More than she ever thought possible.

Chapter Ten

August 4th

Andy laid on his couch in joggers and the T-shirt Jessica slept in. It smelled of her. Of home. The TV was off and the only light in the room came from the moon streaming in through the window. He sat there all day, unmoving. He had since Jessica walked away from him, leaving him broken. In one hand, Andy held a letter from the hospital board of administration. An acceptance of his sabbatical. Two weeks ago Andy applied to take a year off so he could spend every waking moment with Jessica.

It came too late.

In his other hand, Andy held two tickets to Paris. The names read; Mr and Mrs Wilkie.

Jessica.

August 5th

Jessica pressed the side button on her phone, the bright light searing her eyes. Waves of nausea washed over her as she clutched a piece of paper to her chest. Her vision grew darker but she fought against it. She wasn't ready yet.

Just one more day. I have to finish this letter.

August 7th

Jessica wrapped her arms around herself and she spewed more blood from her stomach. She closed her eyes as dark spots filled her vision. She pictured Andy as her breathing became shallow and the beeping in the room slowed down. His earthy brown eyes were the last things she saw before a sense of peace overtook her.

I love you, Andy.

Jessica took her last breath.

Dear Andy.

If you're reading this, then I'm gone. I'm so sorry. I wish things could be different. I wish when I met you that it was because I was clumsy and had a tendency to fall off buses.

I don't regret agreeing to go on a date with you, but everything that I did from that moment on was incredibly selfish. And for that, and so much more, I am so sorry. The day we met was the worst of my life, yet, it was also the best. I met you. Andy, you taught me how to live. To love. And I do love you, Andy. So much. Thank you for making the time I had left amazing.

I suck at goodbyes. How about this, I tell you that I went away and everything is fine and leave it as that, ok? No goodbyes. No tears. I just went somewhere else. I'm not gone. I'm just not around.

I'm sorry if this doesn't make sense, the nurse is helping me and my meds are super amazing. Big thumbs up for morphine.

I love you, Andy. Always. Forever.

Jessica xoxo

Six months later

Andy knelt in the grass with a trowel in his hands. "These ones are pink. It took me forever to find them, apparently, they're rare. They go well with the others." He stood and looked down at the bed of daisies. The wind blew across his face, bringing with it the sweet smell from the flowers. "Your mum is doing good today, she even remembered my name."

He laughed softly and looked up at the sky, "She sends her love. Like she does every day." Tears rolled unchecked down his face, "I miss you so much." Andy kissed the tips of his fingers and laid them on the black and white photo on the gravestone. Moving away, he packed his tools and poured the last of the water over the daisies. "I'll be back tomorrow, love. Sleep tight." Just as he was about to wall away, a beautiful butterfly landed on the stone, its wings gleaming in the light. Andy looked down at his wrist, the butterfly there had a very special meaning to him. "I love you, Jessica."

The end.

?????????????

In loving memory of my Auntie Andrea who lost her battle with ovarian cancer in 2010.

We remember you in every butterfly we see. Xoxo

To my Auntie Barbara. I bet your "kung foo fighting" with balloons up your top in heaven. That's how I'll always remember you. We love you, Babs.

xoxo

To those fighting cancer, you got this! You really have. Kick cancer's arse and show it the door! My love goes to you xoxo

Beat cancer? High fucking five my friend! You badarse! Sending you my love xoxo

To the scientists battling every day to find a cure for cancer, thank you so much. You can do this. Keeping going, please. My love and gratitude xoxo

To those who have bought/read this book, thank you so much. Every penny will be donated to cancer research and proof will be posted in my Facebook group every month around the 29th (please note that royalties are paid in arrears so no royalties will be received for 3 months. From that point on they will be donated as soon as they are received)

I'd like to thank Eileen Troemel for editing this book for free. Love you x

Thank you Trice Ellis of Dream covers by K & L for donating the cover. Love you x

?????????????

Also by Amelia K. Oliver

? COMPLETE SERIES ALERT ?

? The Everly Davis chronicles ?

? COMPLETE BOX SET ?

Get yours here -

https://books2read.com/u/baWeZq

? The Marked for series ?

Marked for Life

https://books2read.com/u/mgZ0Nv

Marked for the hound

https://books2read.com/u/m2VPyO

Marked for Death

https://books2read.com/u/mdzGNl

Marked for Eternity

https://books2read.com/u/bzoW9L
? The Everly Davis chronicles 1-3 ?
https://books2read.com/u/baWeZq
? Blaze ?
https://books2read.com/u/4NQzwo
? Shadows Puppet ?
Dark romance
https://books2read.com/u/mKDEd5
Join my Newsletter for news and updates -
http://eepurl.com/gK6XV1
Stalk me on social media - https://linktr.ee/ameliaoliverauthor

Also by Amelia K Oliver

On the wings of a butterfly

www.ingramcontent.com/pod-product-compliance
Lightning Source LLC
Chambersburg PA
CBHW061447160726
47995CB00003B/1078